As Warm as the Sun

Kate and Jim McMullan

NEAL PORTER BOOKS
HOLIDAY HOUSE / NEW YORK

Toby loved a morning sun puddle,

a lap on a lazy afternoon,

a fire on a fierce night.

But in time,
the sun
faded,

the lap
disappeared,

the fire fizzled out,
and Toby felt
cold and cranky.

At night, Toby dreamed of running,  sniffing, digging,

searching for something
as warm as the sun
that would never
fade or disappear
or fizzle,
but he could
never find it.

One chilly morning,
Toby heard *Woof!*

And in came . . . Pinkie!

Toby circled.

He sniffed.
He pulled
himself up
to show
that he
was the
BIG DOG.

Pinkie trotted over to Toby's sun puddle

and made herself at home.

That wasn't all.

She muscled in on Toby's lap.

She hogged his spot by the fire.

Toby felt pushed out,
left out.

He barked:
WOOF WOOF! GO AWAY!

But Pinkie stayed,

stretching into those warm spots

as if they'd been hers, always.

Maybe
he was
the one
who
should
GO AWAY.

Feeling alone
and forgotten,
Toby curled into
a cold corner.

Toby felt
something
warm against
his rump.

It warmed him
all over
and Toby knew . . .

. . . the something
as warm as the sun
was right there
beside him,

and always
would be.

Pinkie knew
it, too.

In memory of Toby and Pinkie
and for Lily and Arthur

Many thanks to Lincoln Steinkamp as well as Josie Zieger, David Roberts,
and their Frenchie pals, Budos and Moby

Neal Porter Books

Text copyright © 2019 by Kate McMullan
Illustrations copyright © 2019 by Jim McMullan
All Rights Reserved
HOLIDAY HOUSE is registered in the U.S. Patent and Trademark Office.
Printed and bound in July 2018 at Toppan Leefung, DongGuan City, China.
The artwork for this book was made with watercolor.
Book design by Jennifer Browne
www.holidayhouse.com
First Edition
1   3   5   7   9   10   8   6   4   2

Library of Congress Cataloging-in-Publication Data

Names: McMullan, Kate, author. | McMullan, Jim, illustrator.
Title: As warm as the sun / Kate and Jim McMullan.
Description: First edition. | New York : Holiday House, [2019] | "Neal Porter
Books." | Summary: Toby, a French bulldog who dreams of being warm all the
time, is not pleased when Pinkie arrives and takes his favorite warm spots.
Identifiers: LCCN 2018028288 | ISBN 9780823443277 (hardcover)
Subjects: | CYAC: Friendship—Fiction. | French bulldog—Fiction. |
Dogs—Fiction.
Classification: LCC PZ7.M47879 Av 2019 | DDC [E]—dc23 LC record available
at https://lccn.loc.gov/2018028288